Birdseye, Tom.

A tough nut to crack.

$16.95

| DATE | | | |
|---|---|---|---|
| | | | |
| | | | |
| | | | |
| | | | |
| | | | |
| | | | |
| | | | |
| | | | |
| | | | |
| | | | |
| | | | |
| | | | |
| | | | |

# A Tough Nut
# to Crack

## Other Novels by Tom Birdseye

# A Tough Nut to Crack

## Tom Birdseye

Holiday House / New York

Library of Congress Cataloging-in-Publication Data

Birdseye, Tom.
A tough nut to crack / Tom Birdseye. — 1st ed.
p. cm.
Summary: Raised in Portland, Oregon, Cassie adapts quickly
when an emergency brings her family to her grandfather's Kentucky farm,
where she feels the spirits of her mother and grandmother
as she tries to heal the rift between her father and grandfather.
ISBN-13: 978-0-8234-1967-8 (hardcover)
ISBN-10: 0-8234-1967-3 (hardcover)
[1. Farm life—Fiction. 2. Family problems—Fiction.
3. Grandfathers—Fiction.
4. Kentucky—Fiction.]   I. Title.
PZ7.B5213Tou 2006
[Fic]—dc22
2006024887

This book is dedicated with great respect to
Albert "Buster" Holsclaw
and
Rube Kubale

# Contents

# A Tough Nut
# to Crack

# 1. *Whoosh!*

My brother Quinton is eight years old and knows everything.

If you don't believe it, just ask him.

Right now he's educating me on how helicopters fly. "Look, Cassie!" he says, twirling around and around in the kitchen. "They spin like this!"

I turn to Dad, thinking that maybe this time he'll actually set Mr. Know-It-All straight and tell him that helicopters don't spin, their blades do. But Dad is busy whistling as he puts away what's left of the spaghetti and that yummy bread he picked up at the bakery. Besides, he'd probably just laugh. He thinks anything Quinton does is cute beyond belief.

So I let it drop. Because anyway, whether helicopters or their blades spin is not the point. The point is that Quinton is supposed to be helping me scrape the dinner plates and load the dishwasher. And he's not.

Which, I have to admit, is getting to me. I'm just about to call him on it, when the phone rings.

"I'll get it!" Quinton shouts and twirls out of control, crash-landing in the trash can, helicopter butt first.

I stroll over to the phone, taking my own sweet time, smiling. Not because Quinton is sitting in garbage goo with a scowl on his face. But because it's nice to know that even though life isn't always fair, and bad things happen that break your heart, there are perfect moments when people actually do get what they deserve. I scoop up the receiver, cheerful as can be. "Hello, Bell residence."

"Well now, ain't this a sight? I finally got the right number!" The words flow into my ear like syrup, slow and smooth, consonants sounding like vowels, everything rounded. "Clear out there in Portland, Oregon, no less!"

For a second I think it's my friend Katie, putting me on, faking a Southern accent for fun. But then I hear: "You must be Harlan's girl. Cassie, right? Well, honey, I'm a voice from the past, your father's past, to be exact. He around? I need to jaw at him. It's about your grandpa Ruben."

"*Grandpa Ruben?*" I blurt out and instantly regret it. We don't mention that name at our house. Dad won't allow it.

But he's heard me, and it's like someone threw a switch. He goes from light to dark, from chuckling at Quinton the garbage-can man to tight lips and storm cloud eyes. "I'll take it in the bedroom," he says.

I wait until he's on the line and start to hang up. But then I hear that voice again: "Howdy, Harlan. It's me, Vicki Higgins, your old neighbor. Remember? The one who bonked you in the nose with a dirt clod when we were ten?" And I just can't resist. I listen in.

"I hate to rain on your evening parade," Vicki Higgins goes on, "but your daddy's John Deere tractor crashed into my house this afternoon, right through the sliding-glass door, and ended up in my breakfast nook."

Dad takes in a sharp breath. "You okay?"

"Yes, thank the Lord. I was over by the toaster, waiting for a bagel to pop up. Still, it was a bit of a shock. Made me swallow my gum. I yelled at Ruben that he could've at least knocked. But then I realized Ruben wasn't in the driver's seat. No one was."

"Uh-oh," Dad says.

"Uh-oh is right," Vicki Higgins agrees. "I followed the tractor's path of destruction back up the hill, and that's where I found him. . . ."

She pauses, and I can hear her take a deep breath.

"I know you two fell out a long time ago, Harlan, and this is none of my business; but I think you need to come back here lickety-split. You see, when I got to the barnyard, there was your daddy, lying on the ground . . . right where his tractor had run over him."

*Whoosh!* The next thing I know, it's thirty-six hours later; and I'm standing in a place I was sure I'd never be, trying to focus my dazed brain and jet-lagged eyes in the July morning light.

Everywhere I look, all I see is Kentucky.

# 2. The Scene of the Crime

Kentucky. I looked it up in the encyclopedia last year in seventh grade. I know the capital is Frankfort, and the state bird is the cardinal.

And I know they mine coal in the mountains and grow tobacco on the farms, and are famous for racehorses and as the birthplace of Abraham Lincoln.

And I know they are pretty much crazy over basketball, especially University of Kentucky Wildcats basketball.

And I know they call it the Bluegrass State, although I can't figure out why. The grass looks green to me.

Still, reading about a place and looking at pictures is one thing.

Standing in the middle of it is another.

Especially if that middle is the middle of your grandfather's farm. The grandfather you've never met.

I blink and try to take it all in—the old stone house, the vegetable garden, the weathered barn, the smell of hay, the wild chorus of crickets and songbirds, the hot air so thick with humidity the sky is silver instead of blue—but it's just not computing. This Oregon city girl might as well have landed on Mars.

Then I notice the flattened fence and tire tracks, heading down the hill through a field. This has got to be the "path of destruction" Vicki Higgins was talking about. And I just have to follow it. Who wouldn't?

First I check back over my shoulder. Good, the farmhouse sits dark and quiet. Dad's still asleep. Poor guy, he was worn out after the long flight, the delay switching planes in Chicago, the rental car mix-up.

Quinton is snoozing, too, curled into a ball with the pillow over his head, as usual.

If Mom were still alive, she'd be up. And right beside me saying, "Let's see what this is all about, Cassie." I step over the splintered fence planks and into the field.

The grass is covered with morning dew. In seconds it soaks through my running shoes and gives me soggy socks.

I walk on, though, and on, and on down the hill, getting more and more amazed with each step. That a tractor could go so far on its own, as if it were aiming for Vicki Higgins' house. As if Grandpa Ruben had aimed it.

I stop at the thought. No, surely not. No one, not even Grandpa Ruben, would do that.

Or maybe he would. He's not one of those nice grandpas, the perfect kind I'm supposed to have, like in magazines and TV ads. The cold, hard truth is that he's a mean old man and is no doubt one of those rotten neighbors that nobody likes, a farmer Scrooge, who hates everyone and their pets.

Especially everyone who is happy. He probably got mad at Vicki Higgins because she sings while washing her car, or laughs too loudly while sitting on the back porch, and he can hear it all the way up at his house.

So the other day he decided that he'd had it with her. He aimed his tractor straight at her breakfast nook, gave it lots of gas, then bailed out, thinking he'd fake falling off and nobody could blame him for the damage. But he tripped and took a nose dive, and the tractor ran over him.

Which some people would say serves him right, seeing as how he was launching an attack on Vicki Higgins. I know he's the only living grandparent I've got, but no wonder Dad doesn't come back to Kentucky to visit. No wonder he hasn't wanted Quinton and me to meet him. No wonder we can't even mention his name.

Just look at what he did to Vicki Higgins's house. There it is now, couldn't miss it. She's tacked a blue tarp over the hole where her sliding-glass door used to be.

And there is the crime weapon, Grandpa's tractor. The exhaust stack is bent over, and the green paint is scratched off on the side, leaving jagged silver scars. I ease across Vicki Higgins's gravel driveway, eyeing that thing the way a knight would a wounded dragon.

And so at first I don't notice the big ball of feathers sitting on Vicki Higgins's side porch. The big ball of feathers that rustles to life. Finally I catch the movement in the corner of my eye and turn to see that it's a turkey.

I've always liked turkeys, and not just sliced on a sandwich with mustard and mayo. I think they're cute, in an ugly-cute kind of way. "Hey, there," I say, happy to finally meet one in person. I kneel down, holding out my hand like you would for a puppy. "How you doing, turkey?"

The turkey rustles its feathers again and stands up. Wow, it's a hefty one! I had no idea they could get that big. It turns its head my way.

"Come here," I say. "Come to Cassie!"

A strange look flickers in the turkey's dark little eyes.

It gobbles once.

And rampages off the porch right at me.

# 3. Just Like Old Times

The fact that I'm being attacked by a turkey doesn't immediately sink in. To me turkeys have always been bowling-ball birds that strut around gobbling and acting goofy, not feathered maniacs out for blood. Finally, though, the bottom line becomes clear: Reaction needed; run for it!

Which I do, double time.

The turkey is much faster than I ever would have thought possible. As quick as I am on my feet—I hold the Highland View Middle School girls' record in the 100-meter dash, not to mention the anchor position in the 1,600 relay—the turkey stays right with me, pecking at my heels.

"Hey, leave me alone!" I yell and cut a quick left.

The turkey cuts a quick left, too.

I whip around the back of a shiny red car, gravel flying out from under my feet.

The turkey is right on me, gobbling with every peck.

Around and around we go. I reach back and swat at it, but that just makes it madder. It pecks me in the calf, and it hurts like crazy. I jump up on the hood of the car, shrieking, "*Owww!*"

"Tom, no!"

I look up to see a boy charging across the lawn, waving a toothbrush like a sword. Toothpaste foam flies with every word.

"Get back in your pen, you idiot bird!"

In a heartbeat the turkey turns on him and charges at full speed, wings flapping. The boy's eyes go wide. "Uh-oh!" He digs his heels in to stop; but his feet go out from under him, and he plops down on the grass, right in the turkey's line of fire.

A woman in a green dress rushes to the rescue, though, and she's armed with a broom. "That's enough out of you!" she says and takes a swipe at the turkey.

It jumps out of the way, gobbling furiously, but does retreat a bit.

"Back where you belong, Tom, or we'll be talking an early Thanksgiving!" the woman warns. With little sweeping motions she herds Tom Turkey across the driveway. "Go on now, into your pen, or *else!*"

Gate latched, the woman runs her fingers through her hair and lets out a big sigh. "Dang bird. He's enough to make me take up an ax."

Now I recognize the voice, the Southern accent. This, of course, is none other than Vicki Higgins. And suddenly it occurs to me that she might not be too happy to have a member of the Bell family on the hood of her shiny red car, or anywhere near her property, for that matter, even if I never have met Grandpa Ruben, much less driven a tractor. "I'm sorry," I say, easing myself down onto the driveway. "I didn't mean to bother you. I just had to see . . ."

I point to the scene of the crime. Vicki Higgins glances over at her bashed-in house, then back at me. Ashamed at what my mean old grandpa did, I look down.

That's when I notice Vicki Higgins's shoes. High heels. I know it's not the time, but I can't help wondering: How does she keep her balance in those things? Especially on gravel?

"So we finally meet," Vicki Higgins says.

I look up to see her grinning. "Don't worry, honey, I won't bite. I promise. I've had my shots!" And just like that, she's by my side with her arm over my shoulder and guiding me around the boy, who is still plopped in the grass with a stunned look on his face.

"Get up, TJ," Vicki Higgins says to him, "you're drooling."

TJ blinks, then goes red-faced. Frantically wiping toothpaste foam from his chin, he scrambles to his feet. He spins and runs ahead of us into the house, tripping on the doorsill as he goes.

Vicki Higgins laughs. "That boy's a wonder on the soccer field, but can't walk a straight line when he sees a pretty girl."

This catches me by surprise. (Compliments always do.) I fight not to blush, but that's not the kind of thing you can control. I feel my face going hot, like TJ's. Vicki Higgins acts like she doesn't see it, even though I can tell she does. She gives me a pat on the back and ushers me inside.

It's not often I go speechless. But when I see the mess my grandpa made of Vicki Higgins's breakfast nook, all I can do is stand there with my tongue-tied mouth hanging open. It looks like something you'd see on the six-o'clock news, a for-real disaster. If it were my breakfast nook, I'd be mad with a capital M.

Vicki Higgins doesn't seem all that concerned, though. Between swigs of coffee she's putting the milk and cereal away, wiping the counter down, and talking pretty much nonstop about that turkey.

"Crazy old bird thinks he's a watchdog. Got out of his pen for the umpteenth time last week and attacked the UPS truck. Chased it out the driveway, pecking at its back tire. Gonna get run over, if he's not careful. Whoever hits him is gonna have a dent in their fender, though. He's a big one. Weighs close to fifty pounds. Will eat just about anything, except his vegetables. He and TJ are one with the world on that issue. Put a bowl of peas in front of either one of them, and they run like it's buckshot. Old Tom loves lasagna, though, and spaghetti, and cookies. And Trix. Give him a handful of Trix, and I'll swear he grins."

She demonstrates, showing me what I take to be a turkey smile.

I giggle, which she seems to appreciate.

"C'mon, honey," she says, "I'll give you a ride up the hill. It's on the way to work and soccer camp."

She grabs a briefcase and keys off the counter. "TJ!" she shouts. "Hurry up, or you'll be late and have to run extra laps again!" She winks at me. "I'm not a nag but can do an exceptional imitation."

We head back outside, where it's getting hotter by the minute. Tom Turkey has moved into the only shade in his pen, up against the garage, where he's pecking at the ground. He stops and gobbles at me, as if to say, "This is my turf, and don't you forget it!"

Vicki Higgins waves him off. "Crazy old bird!"

TJ races out of the house, lugging his soccer bag. He takes the time to thumb his nose at Tom Turkey but still beats us to the car, where he hops into the back. "You can sit up front," he mumbles to me.

"Thanks," I say loud and clear. No mumbling out of Cassie Bell.

Now that I'm not being chased around and around Vicki Higgins's car, I notice that although it's pretty old, it's still cool, real sporty in fact, like something a teenager would drive. *Mustang* it says on the dash.

Vicki Higgins starts the car, and the CD player blasts out at us, making me jump. "Oops, sorry," she says and turns it down a little bit. "Can't get enough of that classic rock." We roar up a gravel lane to the sound of the Beatles tune "All You Need Is Love," and Vicki Sing-along Higgins.

I catch TJ stealing looks at me in the side mirror but do a good job of ignoring him. Vicki Higgins wheels us around to the front of Grandpa Ruben's house, where we find Dad sitting on the porch swing with Quinton.

His eyebrows go up when he sees me. He stands and walks toward the car. "Quinton and I thought you were still asleep in the upstairs bedroom."

Vicki Higgins is out from behind the wheel and around to meet him before I can even find the door handle. "Howdy, Harlan!" she says, and they shake hands. She introduces TJ, who shakes Dad's hand, too, and calls him "sir."

Dad chuckles at that, which is good to hear. He's been way too serious since the phone call about Grandpa Ruben.

I watch it all, thinking that Vicki Higgins is one of those "can-do" people, full of confidence and energy, just like Mom. She has a way of making you feel like you've known her all of your life, even though you just met. I like it.

Quinton does, too, that's obvious. He's drawn to Vicki Higgins like Tom Turkey to a bowl of Trix, especially after she compliments his favorite T-shirt, the dark blue one with the red lightning bolt across the front.

We're all standing around grinning and talking—"Just like old times!" "Don't look a year older, do I? Ha!" "My, Quinton, but you *are* a big boy!"—until Dad glances at his watch and goes dark again.

He doesn't say a thing. Doesn't need to. It's written all over his face. Time to go visit Grandpa.

# 4. Woo-hoo!

Vicki Higgins is gone in a cloud of classic rock dust, and now Dad can't find the keys to the rental car.

Which is not like him. Normally he's pretty organized. He even folds his handkerchiefs. But this Grandpa Ruben thing has him rattled, that's for sure. He's walking circles in Scrooge's old house (no microwave, no computer, a TV so antique it's *got* to be black-and-white), muttering to himself.

Quinton and I sit at the bottom of the creaky wooden stairs and watch the parade. On Dad's next pass I consider suggesting that maybe we should just forget the whole thing. Maybe not finding the car keys is a sign, like one of those omens you see in movies. The sensible thing to do is go home. Now.

But I keep the suggestion to myself. Dad can be pretty stubborn—no, *really* stubborn—when he's made up his mind about something. And besides, he's already thrown up his hands and grabbed a set of Grandpa's keys off a hook by the back door. "All right then," he says. "So be it. We'll take Esmerelda."

Esmerelda? Turns out that's what Grandpa Ruben calls his ancient Ford pickup truck. It's parked out back next to the garden. Dented and dusty, it looks like it should be in a hunk-a-junkyard. I have to slam the door twice to get it to stick.

Dad turns the key. There is a whining sound, the kind Quinton loves to make, then something like a burp, and the engine rumbles to life.

The gears grind and complain. So does Dad. "Don't see how this rickety thing could be legal." But Esmerelda finally starts to roll and—like it or not— we're bouncing out of the barnyard.

Grandpa Ruben's driveway is long, and lined on either side by big, leafy trees and stout stone fences. Which are actually pretty cool, as far as fences go— no mortar, just flat rocks stacked so carefully on top of one another that they don't fall down. It looks old, really old. I wonder who did the work.

Can't think about that now, though. There are so many potholes Dad can't weave around them all, and it makes for a bumpy ride.

We hit one the size of a refrigerator. It jars us so

badly the glove compartment pops open. Inside there is all sorts of stuff: a stubby pencil, some nuts and bolts, two Snickers wrappers, a bunch of wadded-up receipts, one grease-stained work glove, a crumpled Dr. Pepper can.

And that's just the top layer. I reach in to see what's underneath, but Dad says, "Cassie, mind your own business."

Which, again, is not like him. To set him straight I consider quoting Mom: "Never be afraid to look beyond the obvious." Because that's what I was doing—looking beyond the obvious—trying to find out more about Grandpa Ruben.

Just the thought of Grandpa makes me queasy, though, so I keep my mouth shut. Besides, Dad doesn't like to talk about Mom. I close the glove compartment, twice. Do you have to slam everything around here? Guess so. I let out a big sigh, so Dad will know he's being weird.

Dad acts like he doesn't notice. He's listening to another of Quinton's made-up "facts," this one concerning the speed of light: "Two hundred thirty gazillion miles per second, which is really, really fast!"

Unlike Esmerelda, which is really, really slow. She moves like a slug in mud. Still, we've finally made it to the end of the drive and are pulling out onto the paved county road. Dad gives Esmerelda lots of gas. The speedometer creeps higher. Hot air streams into the windows. It makes me wish for a cool Oregon breeze. Be patient, Cassie, I say to myself. The sooner we go see Grandpa and get it over with, the sooner we go back home where we belong.

A man in a newer truck passes us and waves. Quinton says, "He probably thinks we're Grandpa, huh?"

Dad shrugs. "Maybe, but not necessarily. It's just what folks do around here—wave."

Quinton starts flapping his hand at every car we see. Sure enough, everyone waves back.

It's only a mile or so before we come to the edge of Macinburg, Kentucky. "Population 10,388," the sign says. We pass a Wal-Mart, a shopping center, neighborhoods, and a gas station with a billboard out front that says, "Sam told me to change this sign, so I did!"

Quinton waves at a woman pumping gas. She waves back. We turn right onto a side road, cross some railroad tracks, and swing into the Macinburg General Hospital parking lot.

Dad shuts off Esmerelda. He pulls himself up real

straight, like a soldier getting ready for battle, and takes a deep breath. "Okay," he says, and we march up the sidewalk and through the automatic sliding doors.

It takes a few minutes of waiting at the front desk, but finally we are directed to the fourth floor. Once there Dad points to a row of chairs and says, "You kids wait here. I want to get some information. This may take awhile, so sit tight, okay?"

We say okay and watch him walk over to a big counter, where he starts talking to a nurse. I can't hear what she says, but I can pick up that she has an accent just like Vicki Higgins's.

Quinton catches it, too. He says, "You know why people in Kentucky talk the way they do?"

This isn't a question. It's just Quinton, letting me know that Mr. Know-It-All is about to start lecturing again; more "facts." Too bad my brother didn't come with an ON-OFF switch; I'd duct-tape it in the OFF position.

"It's because they eat so much Kentucky Fried Chicken," he says.

I can't let this one slide. "No it's not. My humanities teacher, Mr. Taylor, loves Kentucky Fried Chicken, and he doesn't have an accent. People here talk like they do because this is the South and people in the South have Southern accents."

Quinton shakes his head. "Dad's from the South, and he doesn't have a Southern accent."

"That's because he moved away a long long time ago. He's lost it."

"No," Quinton says, "that's because he teaches English at the high school, and they won't let him talk like that."

But I'm not listening. There is a strange noise coming from down the hall. "Woo-hoo!" Like a train whistle . . . kinda, sorta, maybe, ish. I'm trying to figure out what might be making the noise, when Quinton notices it, too.

"You know what that is?"

"No, and neither do you."

He starts to protest, but we both are on our feet by then, walking toward the sound. My shoes squeak on the polished tile floor. I go up on tiptoes to quiet them. Because there the sound is again—"Woo-hoo! . . . Woo-hoo!"—louder now.

We ease around the hallway corner and can really hear it. "Woo-hoo!" It's coming from that room there. We creep up to the door and peek in. A stout old woman with curly white hair sits, propped up in bed. She's got a deck of cards and is flicking one after another backhanded at an empty bedpan at her feet, trying to get them in the pan's hole.

"Woo-hoo!" she says.

The old woman has hit a bull's-eye. Her face lights up like the Fourth of July. I can't help but smile, too. She looks like the kind of grandma I read about in books, or see in holiday TV specials—funny, and full of good stories, and nice.

Yeah, really nice, and always there for her grandkids, no matter what. And . . . well, cool in a grandma-cool sort of way, the kind of chocolate-chip-cookie-baking, storytelling, you-can-stay-up-as-late-as-you-want, perfect grandma every kid needs. Just seeing her there laughing in her hospital bed gives me the sudden and powerful urge to run up and hug her. Although I don't. It's not okay to run up and hug strangers, no matter how much you feel like it.

"Woo-hoo!"

She's hit another one. She laughs and claps her hands, then reaches up and pulls her curly white hair off and tosses it in the air.

It takes a second for me to realize that it's not actually real hair, but a wig.

Then another second to see that she's not really an old woman, but an old man.

An old man who's now looking our way. "Woo-hoo!" he hollers and grins from ear to ear.

That's when it hits me. My mouth falls open, and I gasp. It's been a while, but I remember every detail of the photo I found tucked in the back of Dad's dresser. It's of a younger man, with more hair, and not nearly as wrinkled. Still, there's absolutely no doubt about it. *That* is Grandpa Ruben Bell.

# 5. RC Cola and a Moon Pie

"You're so pretty I only need one eye to look at you," Grandpa Ruben says to me, then winks. To Quinton he adds, "And you, my good man, are as rough-and-ready-a-looking kiddo as I've ever seen!"

When we don't react, just stand there dumbstruck in the doorway, he waves the wig in the air. "Don't worry. It's all right. This is fake, but I'm not. Your grandpa just can't resist a little joke, that's all."

Quinton gawks up at me. Evidently he didn't nose around in Dad's dresser looking for photos like I did. "That's Grandpa?" he asks. "Really?"

I'm still in shock—I was expecting a tractor-flattened version of the boogeyman, not a cuddly old guy who could pass for Santa—but I manage to nod.

Grandpa laughs. "Yep, really." He flops the wig back on his head, then off again, then on. "What do you think? Do I look better with or without? Vicki

Higgins gave it to me. She said I didn't have enough hair of my own, which is true. Gave me some Moon Pies, too."

"Moon Pies?" Quinton asks, edging into the room.

"Yep," Grandpa says. "Marshmallows squeezed between graham crackers, then coated in chocolate. Yummy stuff. Vicki Higgins brought me a half dozen to munch on. And an RC cola, of course. Can't have a Moon Pie without an RC cola." He grabs a plastic bag from the bedside table and starts digging around in it. "I drank the RC, but got several Moon Pies left. Y'all want to try one?"

Before I can blink, Quinton is at Grandpa's side, tearing open a clear wrapper and biting into a round Moon Pie. "Yum!" he says.

Grandpa Ruben chuckles and gives Quinton a hug and a kiss on the forehead. "Want a sweet treat, too, Miss Cassie?"

I consider the Moon Pie Grandpa Ruben is holding out. And the kindness in his blue eyes. And the warm, good-natured grin. And the gentle hand on Quinton's shoulder. And my head swims.

A part of my brain is pointing out in no uncertain terms that everything is moving *way* too fast and

I should be *very* careful. This is, after all, the man that my father—a great dad if there ever was one—has disowned.

The rest of my brain, though—and the voice of my mom, there at my shoulder—is arguing just as strongly that I should relax and trust my heart. Because my heart is telling me—no, *yelling* at me—that not only do I want a Moon Pie; but much much more than that, I also want a hug and a kiss on the forehead, just like the one Quinton got.

From my very own grandpa.

As if he can read my mind, Grandpa Ruben says, "You have no idea how happy I am to finally meet you."

The next thing I know, I'm across the room, throwing my arms around his neck. He hugs me back and gives me a kiss on the forehead.

From that close I see happy tears in his eyes. Which gets me watery, too. For a second I'm sure we're both going to start bawling like in a sappy movie, and that would be okay. I happen to *like* sappy movies.

But then Quinton says, "Did you know that caramel is made with bee barf?"

The laugh that bursts out of Grandpa Ruben is the big, openmouthed, throw-back-your-head-and-let-it-loose kind. Which makes me laugh, too. Which gets Quinton going. And in seconds we're all laughing so hard we have to hold our sides.

Finally Grandpa Ruben recovers enough to say, "Why no, I didn't know that. But do you know what you get when you cross a bear and a cougar?"

Quinton gets his breath back and ponders the question for a moment. As much as he hates not knowing everything, or I should say *pretending* like he does, he finally shrugs. "I give up. What do you get?"

"A booger!" Grandpa Ruben says, and we all let loose again.

So it goes. Odd bits of wacky Quinton made-up trivia: "The nearest relative of the panda bear is the hippopotamus."

Goofy Grandpa Ruben jokes: "Where do cows go on Saturday nights? To the moo-vies!"

A bit of leg pulling from me: "It rains so much in Oregon we don't walk to school, we snorkel. We don't tan, we rust!"

Which sets off a string of questions from Grandpa. What is it *really* like in Oregon? More important, what are our lives like there? He wants to know every-thing from A to Z.

In return we get the lowdown on the tractor inci-dent. "Like a fool, I wasn't paying attention," Grandpa explains. "Hit a bump and fell off, simple as that. With no one in the driver's seat, the old John Deere took the opportunity to teach me a lesson, then made a break for it. Vicki's house was the roadblock."

His injuries, thank goodness, are not nearly as bad as everyone first thought. "Sure, I've got a bruised kidney and a cracked rib, and am mighty sore, even with the painkillers they gave me. But the docs are ninety-nine-point-nine percent sure there is no inter-nal bleeding. Plus I got a new hip out of the deal."

"A new hip?" Quinton says. "Wow!"

Grandpa grins like he just won the lottery. "I'll say!" He explains how a surgeon took out the entire top of his right leg bone and put in a man-made replacement, complete with the fancy joint part. "Superglued the old and the new together, no kid-ding! They've already had me up and walking *twice* this morning. Amazing, isn't it? A regular who'd-a-thought-it!"

We talk about what it's like to be in the hospital:

"Very inconvenient," says Grandpa. "The nurses are always checking on me, then talking about me like I'm not in the room. Then they wake me up in the middle of the night to ask if I'm in pain."

He chuckles. "I got them back, though. Told them I'd been doing dance aerobics with a TV exercise show. Is that okay? Then I unplugged the heart monitor and played dead. *Haw!* You should have seen their faces!"

"Go, Grandpa!" says Quinton.

Grandpa shakes his head. "They're still one up on me, though. They make me wear these dang hospital gowns that open in the back instead of the front. Must have been designed by Seymour Butts." He elbows Quinton. "Get it? See . . . More . . . Butts?"

We all laugh again. Quinton wants to know when Grandpa can leave. Grandpa shakes his head. "Gotta stick around a few more days for 'observation.' Doctor's orders. Still, I sure would love to be home this very minute."

We gaze out the fourth-floor window at his farm in the distance: "Over there," he says, "is the road you came into town on, and those lines of trees are on either side of my driveway."

We follow his finger as he points out each detail. "And there is my house. And my garden. Boy-oh-boy, do I miss those fresh veggies. And there with the shiny tin roof is the barn. Across that pasture is the only bit of farming I still do these days—my wheat crop. See it shining golden in the sun? Isn't it beautiful? It's small, only a couple of acres, sown every year in honor of your grandma Chrissy."

Oh, yeah, Grandma Chrissy. Dad carries an old yellowed photo of her in his billfold. She died when he was little. Poor Dad. He lost his mom, then his wife. That's a lot of hurt, twice as much as mine. No wonder he's so quiet about it. Thinking about Grandma and Mom makes him too sad.

Me, I'm just the opposite. I *like* thinking about Mom. When I do, it's as if she's here with me, walking alongside me, giving me advice, helping me figure things out, like a guardian angel.

Grandpa smiles, and I can tell he's remembering Grandma Chrissy. "She loved to bake from scratch," he says, "and insisted that the best bread came from the best grain—hard red winter wheat. I still plant in the fall, the same way we always did, with a hand-cranked seeder. The wheat sprouts, then goes dormant and winters over. Come spring it takes off again like a caged bird set free. It's a sight to behold. A bit of cultivating keeps the weeds down. By June it's got kernels, which are at first pasty, then crunchy, and finally ready to harvest."

"I like bread," Quinton says.

I nod. "Me too."

Grandpa pats both our hands. "Lordy, how I wish your grandma were alive today to meet you two. She'd give you both the biggest hugs in the whole wide world!"

Just him saying it and I can almost feel Grandma Chrissy's arms around me, soft and warm, but strong, too. I've never thought of a wheat crop—or any kind of crop for that matter—as beautiful. But now, looking out the window at it and thinking about why Grandpa planted it, I have to admit that he's got a point. "It's beautiful wheat, Grandpa."

"*Really* beautiful!" says Quinton.

Grandpa Ruben grins from ear to ear. "Woo-hoo!" he says, and plops his wig on top of Quinton's head.

"Woo-hoo!" Quinton says, and dances around the room, holding his half-eaten Moon Pie in the air.

I join in, too, dancing and waving my Moon Pie, and thinking, This is perfect, while Grandpa Ruben claps his hands in delight.

"Woo-hoo! Woo-hoo!" we all are singing, when Dad walks into the room.

# 6. A Tough Nut to Crack

Silence falls like a hammer. Quinton and I lower our Moon Pies and look back and forth between Dad and Grandpa, who are eyeing each other the way most people do pit bulls.

Grandpa finally nods and says, "Hello, Harlan."

Dad nods back, barely. "Hello."

There then follows two minutes of the most meaningless conversation—if you could call it conversation—I have ever heard. Two adult men, father and son, moving their mouths, wagging their tongues, using words to say . . . nothing. Nothing about the tractor wreck. Or Grandpa's hip. Or the not-so-minor fact that they haven't seen each other in just about forever, much less written or talked on the phone. Or *why*. The topic of discussion is— tah-dah!—the weather.

"Hot today."

"Yep, Weather Channel says it'll hit ninety-three."

"Like a steam bath with this humidity."

"Tomatoes will be stewing on the vine."

"That's hot, for sure."

"Mmm-hmm, hot indeed."

The longer this nonsense goes on, the more I can't believe it. How can Dad—the same guy who dances with me in the kitchen, and has endless patience with Quinton—how can he just stand there, like he's talking to a stranger?

And how can Grandpa—who only seconds ago was hugging and kissing and laughing and telling jokes with Quinton and me—how can he suddenly be so grim-faced and steely-eyed with his one-and-only son? I'm just about to shout, "What *is* it with you two?" when Dad says, "Well, I guess we'll head back out to the farm and make sure everything is okay. Let's go, kids." And just like that he's walking out of the room.

As if I have no mind, I fall into line like a good little girl and follow Dad and Quinton into the hall.

Where I finally wake up and screech to a halt. No, I am *not* leaving without at least trying. No way, no how. Mom always said, "Never be afraid to ask the hard questions." I wheel and march right back into

Grandpa's room and just blurt it out. "What happened between you and Dad?"

The surprise on Grandpa's face lasts only a second, then it's gone, replaced by a look I can't read. "Did you know," he says, "that the best chocolate chip cookies are made with real butter?"

Dad is equally helpful in the hospital parking lot. "I could use a cup of coffee," is all he'll say.

Gee, thanks, guys! How enlightening! I might as well ask Quinton. Clearly this Grandpa-Dad thing is going to be a tough nut to crack.

Back at the farm I go for a walk to do some thinking, forgetting that it's too hot to concentrate on anything but the heat. Within seconds sweat is beading up on my forehead and temples. A minute more and it's dripping down my face in salty rivulets.

I hoof it over to a tree-shaded fence line. Which is better, sorta, kinda, maybe, ish. I wipe the sweat off, then wipe it again. No use. Might as well try to hold back the tide. I'm just about to make a dash for the house, where I intend to stick my head in the freezer for an hour or two, when I notice that I'm standing at the edge of a field of waist-high grain.

Grandma Chrissy's wheat.

From the hospital window it was a distant patch

of gold shining in the sun, more an idea than anything real. But now here it is so close I can see each individual plant, rising up out of the dark soil, each strawlike stem, each long, slender leaf, each crowning cluster of kernels.

A slow breeze stirs the tops of the wheat, causing a swishing sound. One seed head brushes against my hand, as if asking to be picked. I do, bring it up to my face, close my eyes, and inhale. And I'll swear it's as if I can smell Grandma Chrissy's bread fresh out of the oven; can hear her voice there by my shoulder, the same way I hear Mom's. "You can figure this out, Cassie," they're both saying. "Your dad and your grandpa may be stubborn, frustrating men at times, but they're worth it; they're family."

"Family," I say, and marvel at the new sound of the word. It may have the same number of letters as always, but now the number of people it includes has grown.

I pick two more clusters of wheat as a gift for Grandpa Ruben before heading back to the house. Don't worry, Grandma. Leave it to me, Mom. I'll have this figured out in no time!

# 7. Yuck!

It's almost midnight, and I'm still wide awake. I've tried everything I can think of to get to sleep: counting backward from five hundred, twiddling my thumbs, meditating on the word *snooze,* even visualizing Mrs. Brookline's algebra class, which has put hundreds of kids into la-la land. No luck. My eyes just keep popping open.

Normally on a night like this, I would turn on the bedside light and read a mystery. If I can't get my zzzzs, I might as well enjoy a good book, and who-done-its are my favorite. But I've already got enough mystery to keep me awake all night long—a real-life mystery: the case of *Dad v. Grandpa Ruben.*

Which, it turns out, is not as easy to solve as I figured, even with Mom and Grandma Chrissy on my side. I've thought and thought and thought about it but have no clue what drove those two apart.

Whatever it was, it probably happened here in this homestead, or at least started here. Wouldn't it be nice if houses came with an account of every event that took place in them, like a captain's log on a boat? I could just flip through the journal and get all the details.

Or while I'm wishing, why not just wish for talking walls. I could say, "Hey, room! What do you know about Grandpa and Dad?" And it would say, "Well, Cassie, it happened like this. . . ."

Or if this particular room didn't know the answer—because it would only know what happened within its sight—it might send me to ask the living room; or the kitchen; or the family room; or across the upstairs hall to the room with the closed door, Grandpa's room. I'd have my answer in no time.

Case solved.

Family fixed.

End of story.

Perfect.

Just . . . like . . . that.

Sure, Cassie, in your dreams. Shaking my head, I finally give up and get up. I walk to the window and look out into the night. There's just enough moonlight to make out parts of the garden, the barn, the—whoa, fireflies! Bunches of them, flashing yellow above the backyard. I've read about them before but never actually seen even one. We don't have fireflies in Oregon.

Seconds later I'm walking out the back door. The air still borders on hot, despite the hour, and is heavy with humidity. The grass feels cool under my bare feet, though. Cricket music is everywhere. The smell of someone's fresh-cut hay hangs in the air. I take a deep breath. Mmm, nice . . .

A firefly blinks on a few feet away at eye level, then blinks off. I ease in that direction and wait. It lights up, close, and I reach out. The firefly goes dark again, but then the glow of yellow pops on as it hovers inches from the palms of my hands. I slowly cup my fingers around it, then open them. The firefly sits there, flashing like a caution light, then slowly lifts off and flies up, winking, into the star-studded sky.

Cool, very cool, an enchanted midsummer's night cool.

Until the kitchen light flicks on, spilling its brightness out the window onto the lawn, and the spell is broken. A cabinet door bangs shut; a chair scrapes the wood floor.

It's probably Dad. He complained about jet lag and sleep problems while we ate our Chinese take-out dinner. Or maybe it's the thought of Grandpa that's keeping him awake, the thing that came between them. This might be a good time to ask again, in the middle of the night. Could be he's ready to talk.

Mom would try, if she were here. Grandma Chrissy, too, I'll bet. They knew Dad as well as anybody. I might as well give it another go. What have I got to lose? I take a deep breath of the warm night air, gather my courage, and walk back into the house, only to find Quinton sitting at the kitchen table, facing a bowl full of Cheerios.

He looks up at me with droopy eyes and says, "I couldn't sleep."

I nod. "I know the problem. Probably thinking about Dad and Grandpa, too, huh?"

"Nope," Quinton says, spooning a big bite of Cheerios into his mouth. "I was thinking about giants, and anacondas, and how to spell *Mississippi* backward. In case you didn't know, it's: i–s–p–i–s–i–p–m–i."

Wrong, I think, but don't feel like arguing the point. I shrug, grab a bowl from the cupboard, and pour myself some Cheerios, too. "Dad asleep?"

"Yep," Quinton says, then flops his head over and does an impression of Dad snoring. "Honk-shoe,

honk-shoe!" He pauses, apparently deep in thought—
if that's actually possible—then says, "I'm going to
play the drums in a band when I grow up. We'll call
ourselves the Concrete Cockroaches."

"Oh" is all I can think of to say, and watch as he
goes back to eating. Weird, weird, weird. What did I
do to be blessed with such a weird brother?

Look at him, sucking on his spoon and gazing up
at the ceiling. He's about to continue his endless
Mr. Know-It-All routine, I can tell. Looking up like
that is a dead giveaway. Next he'll probably tell me
the speed of light. Or the ten grossest things in the
world: number one, slugs; number two, slobbery
kisses from a girl.

Or, no, I bet money he's going to tell me for the
thousandth time how I should never eat bread crust
because it will make me burp. Yep, that's the one,
gotta be. Ha! Am I good or what?

"Grandpa Ruben's birthday is tomorrow," Quinton says.

I eye him for a moment. This point I *will* argue.
"You're making that up."

Quinton scowls. "Am not."

"Are too."

"Am not. I saw it on his bracelet."

"His bracelet? What bracelet? Grandpas don't wear bracelets."

"They do when they're in the hospital, a plastic one. His had his name typed on it and his birthday—seven-thirteen-thirty-four. July thirteenth, that's tomorrow. He'll be . . . seventy-two. I subtracted."

Quinton is actually good at math, I have to give him that, the best in his class. He already knows his timestables. I still don't buy this whole birthday thing, though. I'm a very observant person. I would not have missed a plastic bracelet on Grandpa. "No way," I say.

"Yes way."

"No way."

"Yes way, and if you don't believe me, get a load of the calendar there on the wall."

I glare at him, but then turn and look at where he is pointing. A calendar with a picture of a farm scene hangs near the refrigerator.

"Yeah, right there. July thirteenth."

I step closer and find July thirteenth. In big bold numbers is written, "72!" Below it in smaller letters is scribbled, "And still kicking!"

Okay, so I was wrong, for once. I can handle that. Just as long as Quinton doesn't rub it in by saying—

"I told you so!" Quinton trumpets. "We should have a party."

For an instant I flash ballistic and seriously consider throwing something at him.

Something beefy that would make a really big dent in the little smart aleck's head.

Like the refrigerator.

Yeah, *that* would get his attention. If only I could pick it up.

But I don't even try. Not because it's too heavy, or because I'm too nice a person. I hate to admit it, but I do have a dark side. The reason I stop short of violence is that word Quinton said—*party*—has just now registered in my brain. I look at the calendar again. Seventy-two years old. That's amazing. Grandpa deserves a party. Yeah, a party, with ice cream, and cookies, and *everybody* there.

Everybody, including Dad. Nothing like a party for patching things up.

Like when Stephanie and I got into a fight because I thought she was talking about me behind my back. And we didn't speak for at least two weeks.

But then we both ended up at Anna's birthday party and were roasting marshmallows over the grill in their backyard. Anna's marshmallow caught on fire, and she yanked it out of the flames; it went flying through the air and landed on her dad's hat. He threw it on the ground and stomped on it and dumped his Dr. Pepper on it, too. Stephanie and I laughed really hard and then started talking. And come to find out, she didn't say bad stuff about me at all, and we were friends again.

So anyway, my point is that at a birthday party Dad and Grandpa could patch things up, too. Then we could start acting like a real family, complete with Thanksgiving dinners and Christmas mornings, and picture-perfect family reunion picnics, just like I'm sure Grandma Chrissy would have planned. And Mom, too. She loved picnics! All we need is a party to get the ball rolling. And all we need for a party is someone to organize it. And that someone will be me!

"Yeah!" I say, so excited I completely lose my brain, throw my arms around Quinton's neck, and am all puckered up to plant a big kiss on his cheek . . . when suddenly I regain consciousness.

"Yuck!" we both yell, and jump back. "*Yuuuck!*"

# 8. Timing Is Everything

I'm up by six-thirty the next morning, creeping past Dad's room and down the creaky stairs. No need to wake him again. Last night was enough. I knew it was late—almost one A.M.—but I just *had* to tell him my plan. Besides, I learned a long time ago from Mom that the best time to ask Dad for something is when he's groggy. The groggier the better. Jet lag can be a wonderful thing.

I shook him three times, and finally he sat up in bed. He looked at his watch, blinked several times, then stared at me as if he didn't even know he had a daughter, much less what she was blabbing on and on about.

After I finished telling him about the party and that Quinton is going to draw a picture of concrete cockroaches for a present, but I'm going to give

Grandpa a basket of veggies from his garden and a few stalks of wheat from Grandma Chrissy's field, and those could be from him, too, Dad rubbed his face, looked at his watch again, then at his pillow, then back at me, then he moaned, "If I say okay will you leave me alone and let me sleep?"

I grinned. "It's a deal!"

He was back in snooze-land before his head even hit the pillow.

But anyway, now it's time to get to work. Grandpa Ruben likes chocolate chip cookies. "The best are made with real butter," he had said. No problem, Grandpa. Just so happens they are my favorite, too. Especially when I've got a test to study for. Nothing like chocolate chips to fuel an A. I've baked dozens.

Gotta have the right ingredients, though. I hit the kitchen full stride and start rummaging. As if Grandma Chrissy is guiding me, within minutes I've found everything I need, even my favorite brand of chocolate chips. Perfect!

Perfect, that is, if Quinton would stay out of my hair. No such luck. He's awake and has wandered in to help himself to one of Grandpa's carrots, dipped in ketchup.

Yes, a carrot, dipped in ketchup.

He's doing it to bug me, of course, because I almost kissed him last night. And because bugging me, as he always says, "is fun!"

To top off the carrot and ketchup tactic, he begins to sing. It's one of his original compositions. I don't get all of the lyrics, but do pick up enough to understand that it's mainly about a kid who wakes up to find himself turned into a slice of pizza.

This is bad enough, especially the part where he gets eaten by concrete cockroaches, until you consider the quality of Quinton's voice. Which is . . . how should I put it? Imagine a cross between a dying frog and fingernails on a chalkboard, and you get the idea. It's not music; it's a form of torture.

But I'm in a good mood, what with the party, and Dad and Grandpa about to make up. I keep mixing cookie dough and politely ask Quinton to lay off the squawking, "if you don't mind."

He stops, dips his carrot into the ketchup, and says, "Okay, Cassie," being sure to afford me a stunning view of all the chomped-up carrots and ketchup in his mouth. Then he starts humming. "Mmm-mmmm-mm-mm-m-m-mmmmm . . ."

I begin plopping nice cookie-sized spoonfuls onto the baking sheet I found in the drawer under the oven. I ask Quinton to stop humming. "Pretty please, I've got work to do."

"Okay, Cassie," he says again. To my amazement he actually goes quiet.

For two seconds. "Because now it's time for dessert!" he crows and jams his hand into the mixing bowl, scooping out a big glob of dough.

I grab for him. "Quinton, no!" But he's quick. He darts out of the kitchen, cramming cookie dough into his mouth as he goes.

"Come back here!" I yell. "Those are for Grandpa's party!"

Quinton laughs and sprints down the hall and out the front door. I race after him, gaining with each footstep, and am reaching rocket-ship speed by the time I fly out onto the porch.

Where I smack *slam-blam* into TJ Higgins, who is standing there with a clump of daisies in his hand. He goes sailing backward off the porch in a shower of flowers. He lands in the grass with a thud.

"Oh, I'm sorry!" I blurt out and rush down the steps to help him up.

He waves me off. "I'm okay," he says. "No problem." He's beet red and scrambling to his feet. He scoops the daisies up and thrusts them at me. "Here! I'm sorry about Tom Turkey!"

He tries to smile, but it doesn't work. More like a grimace, really. "It was my fault he got out and chased you. He chases me all the time, too. He's psycho, a mutant monster. They'll make a movie about him some day, *Attack of the Mutant Monster Turkey*. I should have locked him in his pen better."

I don't know what to say. I just stand there. Which seems to make TJ even more nervous.

"Anyway," he says, pushing the daisies at me again. "Here. These are for you."

I don't know what to do, either. No one has ever given me flowers, much less a boy. So I take them, and smell them like girls do in the movies, and sneeze so hard that snot goes flying. TJ jumps back and falls down again. Quinton, who is over by the bushes licking his fingers clean, laughs and laughs and laughs until he falls down, too.

## 9. A Picture Is Worth a Thousand Words

"Surprise!"

Quinton and I burst into Grandpa's hospital room, leaving Dad in the doorway.

Propped up in bed, looking out the window, Grandpa lights up like Las Vegas. "Well now! Looka' who's here!"

"We brought you presents!" Quinton gushes, unloading the goodies into Grandpa's lap. "See?"

Grandpa oohs and ahhs over the artwork, even after Quinton explains that they are concrete cockroaches, not birds.

From the garden basket Grandpa selects a cherry tomato and pops it into his mouth. "Mmm-mmm," he croons.

But it's the stalks of wheat that clearly mean the most to him. He turns them this way and that, nodding, smiling. "Almost time for harvest," he says. "But there's only one way to tell for sure."

He rubs one of the seed heads between his palms, gently at first, then harder. "Now watch this," he says. He opens up his hands and with a quick puff of air—*poof!*—blows the chaff away. Like a magic trick, all that's left behind are grains of wheat.

Grandpa hands a kernel to me and one to Quinton. "Stick it back between your teeth and bite down," he says.

We do.

"It's crunchy!" Quinton says.

Grandpa nods. "That's a good sign. If it were pasty or soft, we would still have a week or two to wait, or maybe even three. The longer you wait, the more there is that might go wrong: disease, not enough rain."

A shadow passes over his face. "Or too much rain. I've seen storms pound healthy wheat flat, soak it swollen and moldy, destroy the entire crop in a matter of seconds."

I shudder. Mom died on a stormy day. Pounding rain still makes my heart ache.

Grandpa holds another of the wheat heads up

and turns it in the light. "But this is as healthy, fine as can be."

"Mighty fine, indeed!"

We look up to see Vicki Higgins hooking Dad's elbow in hers and pulling him into the room. "How nice to see *all* of y'all together!" she says. She winks at me, and I can tell that she's on to my plan. It's like I've got a whole team on my side: Mom, Grandma Chrissy, and now Vicki, too. Which is fine with me. You can't have too many guardian angels.

TJ is with her and seems to have recovered from our last encounter. He ventures a smile at me but keeps his distance, even when I unveil my chocolate chip cookies and the ice cream we picked up at Kroger.

"Ah, cookies and ice cream," Vicki Higgins says. "Good idea, Cassie. Cakes are too much trouble. I baked a fancy one with vanilla icing and red sprinkles for TJ's birthday last year. You remember that, TJ?"

TJ looks at her as if he'd pay a thousand dollars to change the subject. But Vicki Higgins doesn't. She's on a roll.

"Only problem with the sprinkles," she says, "was that they spilled all over the table. So I got out the vacuum cleaner to tidy up. TJ accidentally bumped my elbow. And the next thing I knew, I'd vacuumed up half his cake. Oh, Lordy, you should have heard that boy whine!"

"Mo-om!" TJ protests. "I didn't whine!"

Vicki laughs. "Okay, okay. He didn't whine."

"Shoot, I'd whine if my birthday cake got sucked up in the vacuum," Grandpa says. "Me and vacuum cleaners don't get along. Got my big toe caught in one not more than a month ago. Hurt like the dickens!" He eyes the ice cream. "What kind is it?"

"Mocha almond fudge," I explain. "We spoon it between the cookies and make the ultimate ice cream sandwich!"

Everyone smiles at the thought. Especially Quinton. "Did you know," he informs us, "that vitamins are in ice cream but not in spinach?"

Grandpa puts a hand on Quinton's shoulder. "What you say we tough it out and have two servings then?"

"Yes!" Quinton crows. "I'm hungry all over!"

"Me too," Grandpa says, rubbing his belly.

"Gotta sing the birthday song before we eat," Vicki insists.

Quinton belts out, "Happy Birthday to you, you live in a zoo, you look like a monkey, and smell like one, too!"

Grandpa fakes hurt feelings. "Why does everyone always pick on me?" he whines, then actually squeezes out a fake tear.

Vicki Higgins hoots with laughter and claps her hands. "Bravo!" We all join in the applause, even Dad. Grandpa Ruben gets out of bed—just to show us that he can—and takes a bow.

We make ice cream sandwiches, then crown them with bunches of candles. Grandpa snuffs them all out in one breath and says, "This is the only food you can blow on, and people will still rush to get some."

Quinton scrunches up his face and says, "Yuck!" but is first in line to grab the biggest ice cream sandwich.

"Seventy-two years old!" Grandpa says. "That's a lot of years!"

Vicki Higgins says getting old is more a matter of attitude than numbers.

Dad chuckles and says, "When you start talking like that, it's a sure sign you're getting old."

Vicki laughs. "Takes one to know one, Harlan!"

We all eat and chat at the same time, which makes me grin all the more. It's working! My party plan is working. Just like I imagined!

As if she can read my mind, Vicki Higgins pulls one of those tiny digital cameras from her purse. "Okay, you members of the Bell family," she says. "Line up and try to look presentable. Cassie, you stand by Ruben. Harlan next to her. That's it. Quinton? Where's Quinton? Oh, there you are! Is that your second ice cream sandwich? Or third? Whatever, would you be so kind as to put it down for a moment and get in the picture? Let's see. On the other side of your grandpa would be good."

We follow directions. Vicki Higgins nods approvingly, then looks in the viewfinder and has us scrunch in some more. I put one arm over Grandpa's shoulder, the other around Dad's waist. I squeeze, and they both squeeze back.

"Big smiles!" Vicki Higgins says.

But I can't smile any bigger. My face is already too small to hold a grin a mile wide.

"Woo-hoo!" says Grandpa.

"Woo-hoo!" I sing back and plant a big kiss on his cheek. Perfect!

It isn't until later, after the party is over and we're done cleaning up the mess, that I get the camera from Vicki for a look at the group photo. The camera screen is small, so I have to squint to see everyone's face. Slowly my eyes adjust, bringing detail into focus. There is the Bell family: Quinton, then cheesy me sandwiched in between my grandpa and my dad.

That's when it hits me. The photo may be tiny, but it doesn't lie. All that time Grandpa and Dad were just going through the motions of getting along, acting like they were enjoying each other's company.

To please me.

The smiles on their faces are as fake as fake can be.

# 10. Karate Weed Chopper

Later, back at the farm, the initial sensation of being slapped eventually fades.

Only to be replaced by an hour or so of righteous indignation.

Which, in turn, is followed by a supersized helping of self-pity, wishing I could just fast-forward life the way you can a DVD.

Finally I decide enough is enough. Wallowing in a funk isn't going to help me figure out this Dad-Grandpa thing. Time for a bit of what Mom liked to call "work therapy," which is just a fancy way of saying, "Go sweat it off."

I march out to the garden, where I find a hoe leaning against the shed. I pick it up. I jiggle it in my hands, feel the weight, the balance, how it's made for digging out weeds.

Of which there are quite a few, now that I take a

good look. They're growing between the plants, threatening to take over Grandpa Ruben's veggies.

Oh yeah? Not if I have anything to do with it. I raise the hoe and—*whack!*—bring it down with a satisfying thud. A clump of weeds comes loose. I grab it by the hair, then toss it over the fence.

"And don't come back!" I yell after it.

I raise the hoe, higher this time, and let fly again. *Whack!* Take that! Another weed bites the dust. Over the fence it goes, too.

Really getting into it now, I chop and chop away. *Whack!* Take that! *Whack!* And that!

Weeds are dying and flying. Look out, here comes Cassie Bell, karate weed chopper. She's got power. She's got accuracy. She's got a black belt in weed chopping.

*Ka-whack!* I bring the hoe down with all my might. *Whack!* Man, that feels good! I should do this more often. *Whack! Whack! Wha*-yikes! I've come within a split hair of taking out one of Grandpa's tomato plants.

"Good grief, Cassie!" I say, smacking my forehead with the palm of my hand. "Watch what you're doing!"

I take a deep breath, refocus my weed-whacking energy, and raise the hoe—

"You chop weeds just like your grandmother."

"Eeek!" I jump and whirl around to see Dad leaning on the garden fence, one foot up on the bottom rail.

He's smiling.

I drop the hoe like it's a smoking gun. "Uh, really?"

Dad nods. "She gave everything she did one hundred percent, and was not easily intimidated." He cocks his head. "Did I ever tell you about the time she tossed a raccoon out of the kitchen?"

"Tossed a raccoon?" I say, relieved we're not going to discuss the near beheading of Grandpa's tomato plant. "No. What happened?"

Dad smiles again. He loves telling stories. "I was about five years old," he begins. "Mom and I were in the living room one summer evening—an evening a lot like this—reading *The Cat in the Hat* by Dr. Seuss. We were at the part in the story where the cat and Thing One and Thing Two are going wild, tearing up the house, when we heard a real-life crash in the kitchen. We jumped up and ran in to see a raccoon on the counter, helping itself to the fresh homemade bread your grandmother had just taken out of the oven and left there to cool."

"How did the raccoon get into the house?" I want to know.

"We'd left the door ajar, I guess," Dad says. "Or maybe not. Raccoons are smart and great climbers. Could be it shimmied up the downspout and crawled in the window. All I know for sure is that if it thought this was going to be a cakewalk to a free meal, it had another thing coming. Your grandmother was *very* proud of her baking, and didn't take kindly to uninvited guests. 'Leave my bread alone!' she yelled. She grabbed a broom from behind the door and jabbed it at the raccoon the same way a warrior jabs a spear. But that dang raccoon was an ornery one. It locked hold of the broom straw like a furry demon. Mom shook and shook the broom, but the raccoon wouldn't let go. So she wound up like a baseball pitcher and flung it all—broom and attached raccoon—clean out the kitchen door and into the backyard."

"Whoa!" I say.

Dad nods. "Yep. Like I said, raccoons are smart.

It only needed one lesson to learn not to mess with your grandmother." He chuckles and shakes his head, and I know he can see it all in his mind as if it were happening right now. That's the great thing about a story. It brings the past, and people, alive.

I can see it, too, my wonderful, no-nonsense Grandma Chrissy bouncing that rascal raccoon out of her kitchen. "I'm glad I'm like her," I say. "I just wish I had known her."

"I wish you had, too," Dad says, sadness welling up in his eyes. But he takes a deep breath and swallows hard, and that's the end of that, like always. Back to normal he reaches down and pulls off a long piece of grass and starts chewing on one end, looking like . . . well, looking like a farmer.

Which catches me by surprise. I've never thought of him that way. To me he's always been Harlan Bell, Oregonian, high school English teacher, Dad. But standing here where he grew up, telling a story about his mother, then chewing a piece of grass, it's as if a whole other part of him has suddenly come into focus: Harlan Bell, Kentucky farm boy.

I'm mulling over that historical fact, when Dad's cell phone rings, and just as quickly as it surfaced, the farmer part of him disappears. In one quick urban-man motion, he pops the phone off his belt, flips it open, and answers, "This is Harlan." He listens for a moment, then his eyes cut to me. "Sure, she's right here." He hands the phone my way. "It's for you. An invitation."

I stop short. An invitation? From who? Uh-oh, probably TJ. What if he wants to come visit? Bring more flowers? Or, worse yet, wants me to go somewhere with him? I look to Dad for hints, but he's not helping.

"It's okay with me," is all he says.

I take the phone and raise it toward my ear like it might explode, thinking fast, thinking of excuses. "Hello?"

It's a Higgins, all right, but—whew!—not TJ. "Hey, Cassie, it's me, Vicki. I'm wondering if you'd be interested in getting together for a little chat, just the two of us, you know, woman to woman."

Woman to woman. I like the sound of that. It makes me feel . . . grown-up.

"I didn't tell your dad this," Vicki Higgins goes on, "but the subject of discussion I have in mind is him and your grandpa. Over breakfast tomorrow would work best for me. There's a fun café downtown called the Early Bird. Pick you up at eight o'clock. What do you say?"

What do I—who clearly need all the help with this Dad-Grandpa thing I can get—what do I say?

Hmm, let me think about it . . . for a nano-second.

I say, "Perfect! See you then!"

# 11. Let's Hear It for Ignorance

"Yep, your granddaddy was wild, but your daddy was even wilder," Vicki Higgins says as we barrel down the farm lane, dust flying, then whip onto the road to town. She's almost yelling to be heard over the classic rock tune—"Love Potion Number Nine"—but I don't mind. Three minutes in the car and already I've learned three new things about Dad and Grandpa. At this rate I'll know *everything* by the time we've ordered breakfast!

"Wilder, like on his thirteenth birthday when Harlan tried to ride a bull in the pasture behind the house," Vicki Higgins goes on. "It threw him right over the fence. Which is a good thing. It's nice to have a fence between you and an angry bull. Still, it was impressive to watch. Or insane, depending on your point of view. Men can be real idiots, as you may have noticed."

"Mo-om! I'm not stupid!"

It's TJ from the backseat. We're giving him a ride to soccer camp. He's been very quiet, stealing looks at me in the side mirror, until now.

Vicki Higgins laughs. "I didn't say stupid. Generally you male types have plenty of intelligence. I said *idiots,* as in no common sense. And anyway, I also said men, which you are not . . . yet." To me she whispers, "Lord help us when he becomes a man!"

"Hey, I heard that!"

Vicki laughs again as she pulls into the middle school parking lot. "Okay, my *man,* exit here for soccer camp!"

TJ scrambles out of the car. I can see he's both angry and embarrassed at the same time. He glares at Vicki.

Her face softens when she sees she's pushed it too far. "Oh, honey, you know I love you, and think you're wonderful. Don't be like most men and get riled so easily."

"I'm not riled," TJ shoots back, obviously . . . riled.

Vicki leans out the window and blows him a two-handed kiss, then strikes a rock star pose and croons along with "Love Potion Number Nine."

It works. TJ laughs, despite himself. I should have brought a pen and paper for taking notes. Vicki really does know how to handle guys. This is going to be the most educational breakfast of my life!

The Early Bird Café is small and simple: three rows of tables, a long counter with stools that spin, and slow fans turning overhead. A sign by the cash register says PLEASE SEAT YOURSELF, so we do just that.

"How about over there in the corner," Vicki suggests. "Then we can see all the goings-on while we chat."

Vicki's high heels click on the linoleum floor as we thread our way through the tables. She greets people. "Howdy, Debbie." "Morning, Kelsey, Amy." "How's it going, y'all?" Everyone seems happy to see her.

She introduces me to an elderly couple—Buster and Geraldine—who are sitting side by side with their elbows touching. And a group of men—Stanley, David, and Jerry Michael—who are rolling dice to see who pays for the coffee. And a woman—Brenda—who is picking sesame seeds from between her teeth. They all are glad to meet me and full of sympathy for Grandpa Ruben, especially Brenda. "You tell that old rascal to get well soon, ya hear!"

I promise I will, and thank her.

Finally Vicki and I sit down. A man named Pete, the owner of the Early Bird, comes over and brings us menus, then takes our orders. On his recommendation I go for the ham and cheese omelet with hash browns, and orange juice. Vicki insists on the Dieter's Special—"Even though I'd rather have bacon!"—and coffee—"Strong, like I prefer my men."

This gets a laugh out of Pete. "Vicki Higgins," he says, "you are something!"

I agree. Watching her is like watching a master at work. She's got the gift of understanding people, just like Mom, and Grandma Chrissy, too, I'll bet. She's bound to know exactly what's going on with Dad and Grandpa, and what to do about it.

After Pete brings our drinks and leaves, Vicki tells me about the car wreck Pete was in five years ago. He was hurt bad and would have died if it weren't for Charlie, a local plumber who happened upon the scene and stopped the bleeding until the ambulance arrived. Since then every time Charlie comes in for food, Pete won't let him pay for his meal. Charlie says he was just doing what anybody would have done and keeps shoving money at Pete. No way. Pete shoves it right back and says, "No charge!" They'll probably be at it forever. Neither one will give up.

"That," Vicki Higgins says, "is male stubbornness at its best, both of them sticking to what they think is right." She pushes her auburn hair over her shoulder, and I notice her dress is exactly the same color. No accident there. Vicki Higgins is as classy as she is smart.

"Then there is the other kind of stubbornness," Vicki continues, "that trumps the good kind ten to one. Like stubbornly refusing to put dirty socks in the laundry basket, even after being asked three thousand times. Or jumping to conclusions, then stubbornly ignoring evidence to the contrary. Or pride, that stubborn male I-refuse-to-back-down kind of pride that ends marriages and starts wars, or just plain leads to trouble." She shakes her head. "My ex was particularly good in that department. Poof! Thirteen years of him and me down the drain."

She stops to stir her coffee, and for a moment it's as if the wind has gone out of her sails.

But Vicki Higgins will have none of that. She takes a deep breath, sits up straight, and smiles. "I will admit that the stubborn streak in men *can* be entertaining. For example, do you know that in high school your daddy ate one hundred and three prunes just because a friend bet him he couldn't?"

I go pie-eyed at the number. "One hundred and three? Really?"

Vicki nods. "He paid the price . . . for two days!"

"Ugh!" I say.

Vicki agrees. "Yep. Can't put all the blame on Harlan, though. Stubbornness is hereditary. He got it from your grandpa, who *still* refuses to switch to daylight savings time. He finds it a silly nuisance to reset his clocks twice a year, so the rest of the world can go jump in the lake as far as he's concerned."

We're laughing at that when Pete brings our food. Yummy. We dig right in. Vicki insists I try her cantaloupe. "It's to die for, honey."

I finally talk her into sampling my omelet. "Well, okay," she says, "if it will make you happy. But just a little bite."

She closes her eyes while she chews, a look of pure bliss on her face. She giggles when she opens her eyes again and sees me staring.

"I'm not proposing that women are incapable of stubbornness," Vicki says, picking up where she left

71

off. "Lord knows we are, me in particular. But having admitted as much, it's still men who have the corner on the market . . . by a long shot."

She stops and helps me get ketchup out of the bottle and onto my hash browns, showing me how to thump the bottle in just the right place.

"Which is why, given the stubborn nature of your father and grandfather, I suggested we get together and talk. I have some advice concerning that dilemma, if you're interested."

I stop, a fork full of ketchup-loaded hash browns halfway to my mouth. *Interested?* This is Vicki Higgins talking. Lay your wisdom on me! I take a deep breath and wait, literally on the edge of my seat.

Vicki Higgins purses her lips and looks me over thoughtfully. Finally she begins. "I took a good gander at that birthday photo, too, especially after I saw the effect it had on you. I downloaded it onto my computer and blew it up good-sized so my middle-aged eyes could be sure before I judged. One glance was all it took. No mistaking bad acting, is there?"

She doesn't wait for me to respond. No need. We both know the answer. Dad and Grandpa were faking it for my sake. The party solved nothing. What I need to know now is why. And how to fix it. What next?

As if she can read my mind, Vicki Higgins nods. "I've known both your daddy and your granddaddy a *very* long time, and so, of course, have wondered about their . . . um, 'relationship,' or lack thereof."

She pauses and flicks a grain of salt with her fingernail. "I'm not one to easily give up, Cassie. But I'm not one for beating my head against the wall, either, and I hate to see someone doing the same. Especially someone as smart and wonderful as you."

Vicki Higgins reaches across the table and lays her hand on mine. "Despite any theories I may have entertained, the truth is that I have absolutely no idea what really happened between those two men. Worse yet, I'm not sure if I want to know. I love them both and would like to continue doing so. I'm afraid if I learn the nitty-gritty, it'll send me into a tailspin."

She sits up straight and takes a deep breath. "Bottom line is this: Sometimes there are things in life that are better left alone, and it is my distinct impression that your dad and grandpa's relationship is one of them. My advice to you is to let sleeping dogs lie. As much as I hate to say it, in this case, honey, ignorance is most likely bliss."

# 12. Detective Cassie Bell

All the way home I put on a front of being civil, but the truth is I'm getting madder by the minute. There I was, absolutely positive that Vicki Higgins would have all the answers, and all I got was her telling me to quit.

*Quit?* I'm no quitter! By the time she drops me off at Grandpa's, I'm on the verge of a tizzy fit. All wound up I march into the kitchen, ready to confront Dad. Time for some straight talk around here, father to daughter, no holds barred. I want answers, and I want them *now*!

The kitchen is empty. On the table is a note:

*Quinton was getting a bit stir-crazy. I've taken him fishing at Tank Pond. Be back in a couple of hours. I've got the cell, so call if you need anything, or want to join us. We'll come get you!*

*Love, Dad*

Fishing? At a time like this? Really burning now, I turn and stomp out of the kitchen and up the stairs.

Where I find myself facing the door to Grandpa's room.

The closed door, just like it's been since we got here.

The next thing I know I've got my hand on the doorknob. I expect it to be locked, but a quick twist says otherwise. The door swings open, and before I have a chance to talk myself out of it, I walk inside.

Grandpa's room is small, filled mostly with an old four-poster bed and dresser made of dark wood. A cane rocker is squeezed in beneath a single lace-curtained window. It looks like a display in a museum, something out of the past.

Which it is, of course—Grandpa's past.

Which is exactly what I need to figure out. The full and complete answer to the Dad-Grandpa dilemma is probably right here in front of me, in this very room.

Sure, it's Grandpa's, and so technically I shouldn't nose around. But this is for his own good, and Dad's, and the whole family's. How are we ever going to have fun together like Grandma Chrissy and Mom would want, if someone doesn't solve this mystery and fix it?

Simple: We won't. So somebody has to do something. And that somebody is none other than Detective Cassie Bell!

First stop? Dresser, of course. That's where Dad keeps his important stuff, in the bottom drawer, back right-hand corner. Like father, like son, is my guess. I pull Grandpa's bottom drawer open and find . . . work pants, jeans mostly, the bib-overall kind, just the sort of clothes you'd expect an old farmer like Grandpa to wear.

Hmm, next drawer up? T-shirts neatly folded, mostly white, but not all. Here's a blue one that says "Kentucky Wildcats" across the front, and a green one advertising John Deere tractors, and a kind of melon-colored one that says "Old Fart" in big block letters.

Ha! You gotta love the guy.

Okay, moving right along. Top right-hand drawer holds socks. Lots of socks. Some of which, I notice, need mending or a short trip to the garbage.

Last drawer . . . I slam it shut quicker than a blink. It's full of underwear, and at least one pair of boxers has Donald Duck all over them. There are some things a granddaughter just shouldn't know about her grandpa, and his choice of underwear is one of them.

I shake off the Donald Duck image and head for the closet. Sure, why didn't I think of that first? Closets are where lots of people hide their secrets.

Grandpa's is crammed—work shirts, dress shirts, sweatshirts, slacks, and one Sunday suit and tie. Farmer boots are lined up across the bottom, along with sneakers, two pairs of shiny dress shoes, and even a pair of sandals. Interesting stuff, yes. You can learn a lot about somebody from just looking in their closet. But no help where I really need it.

I shut the closet door and survey the room. Under the bed? That's one of my favorite storage areas, right after the floor, which I consider to be one big shelf. Maybe Grandpa keeps stuff there, too. I drop to my knees and find . . . nothing but dust bunnies.

Hmm, maybe I'm on the wrong track. Maybe I should look in another room, Grandpa's farm office, for example, or the living room, or—

*Screech!* Hold up, Cassie, what's this? A wooden box under the bedside table. I scoot across the floor and pull the box out into the rectangle of sunlight from the window.

The box is no larger than one for shoes, and plain and simple, worn by age. A tiny metal latch holds it closed. I unclip the latch, and the lid pops open . . .

. . . to reveal a man and a woman, smiling up at me from an old, yellowed photo. They're standing side by side. Their faces are young, but I recognize them just the same. Grandpa has his arm over Grandma Chrissy's shoulder. She has hers around the back of his waist. They look so comfortable together, the perfect couple, standing together in front of a field of wheat.

I lean closer and can see that the crop looks ready to harvest. "What fine grain it will be!" Grandpa must be saying. Grandma Chrissy no doubt agrees. "It'll make the best flour and the most delicious bread."

I can almost smell the fresh loaf, just out of the oven, almost feel a warm slice in my hand, almost taste that first bite.

Yum . . .

With a sigh I set the photo aside to see what's next. Whoa! Grandpa in a military uniform. He looks *really* young. I turn the picture over, and there in neat cursive is written "Ruben Bell, July 1952, U.S. Marines, South Korea."

So Grandpa fought in the Korean War. I didn't know that. I look back in the box to find two medals. One is gold and black, and shaped like a heart. In the center is the profile of George Washington, like you see on a quarter. It's hanging from a purple ribbon. The other is a silver star, fixed to a red, white, and blue ribbon. Beside them lies a newspaper clipping.

The article is so old and yellow I'm afraid it will fall apart if I pick it up. I lean close and read. . . .

Hey, it's about Grandpa! Right there it says— "Sergeant Ruben Bell"!

Wow! He was fighting on a hill near a place in Korea called Panmunjom when two of his men were wounded. Under heavy enemy fire he dragged them both to safety . . . get this . . . with a bullet in his leg. "Sergeant Bell would simply not give up," the article says. The medals are the Purple Heart, for being wounded, and the Silver Star, for *gallantry in action*. My grandpa was a hero!

Wait a minute. So Grandpa was a hero in the Korean War and Dad . . .

Uh-oh. Dad really doesn't like violence. He gets upset if I even *look* like I'm going to whack Quinton, no matter how much Quinton deserves it. At the high school Dad sponsors a club called Students for Peace and Global Responsibility. His heroes are people who tried to make the world a better place in *non-*violent ways, like Ghandi, and Martin Luther King, and Mother Teresa, and the Dalai Lama, not generals.

Or sergeants.

That's got to be it, then! Dad and Grandpa argued over Grandpa being a soldier. And Grandpa got mad, then madder. And Dad got madder still. And said he didn't want to be a farmer. And left and ended up in Oregon. Where he couldn't help harvest Grandma Chrissy's wheat. Which made Grandpa even madder. Until they couldn't even talk on the phone without arguing. So they stopped communicating altogether. And here we are today.

I get up and pace the floor, back and forth, back and forth. Okay, so it's a lot to overcome. But they can do it. They've got to. Otherwise, what? We go back to Oregon, and that's it, no real family like the one I'm supposed to have?

No way. I've got to do something. But *what?* I pace the floor some more, and it hits me: Get those two bullheaded men together and *make* them talk it out. Now!

A girl with a mission, I grab for the old black phone sitting on the bedside table. It's one of those old rotary-dial types. But it works. I crank the numbers and within seconds Dad's cell is chiming away.

*Ring, ring.*

I'll get those two talking.

*Ring, ring.*

Then I'll start patching it all up.

*Ring, ring.*

C'mon, Dad, it's Cassie, who is going to make everything perfect!

*Ring, ring.*

*Finally* he answers. "This is Harlan."

"Get to the hospital right now!" I yell into the phone.

Worry jabs into Dad's voice. "What is it?"

"It's an emergency!" I say. "Meet me there!"

And before he has a chance to say another word, I've hung up the phone and am sprinting down the stairs and out the front door.

# 13. Falling Right and Left

I'm halfway to town before it hits me.

The heat and humidity, that is. Whew! You'd think I'd learn. This is not Oregon, Cassie. This is Kentucky, the land of sweat. Rivers of it are streaming down my face, stinging my eyes and tasting like salt. My heart is pounding in my ears. The world is starting to go all fuzzy and white, and my head is swimming.

So it takes a moment to realize that a red Mustang has pulled up alongside me and someone is calling my name.

"Hey, Cassie, where's the fire?"

It's Vicki Higgins, shouting across a wide-eyed TJ in the passenger seat. She's smiling, but even through the fog of my oncoming heat stroke, I can see she's concerned.

"I'm about to faint just watching you run," she says. "Want a ride?"

I try to remind myself that I'm ticked off at Vicki for advising me to call it quits with Dad and Grandpa. But it's too dang hot to stay angry. And the air-conditioned coolness floating out of the open car window is just too delicious to ignore.

"Boy, would I," I say, and dive into the backseat.

Minutes later we're walking through the door of Macinburg General Hospital and onto the elevator. Vicki, to her credit, is biting her tongue and not riddling me with all the questions I can see she's dying to ask. As the elevator door opens onto the fourth floor, she leans close and whispers, "Whatever you've got going, Cassie, I'm on your side, and I'm here if you need me."

Like Mom and Grandma Chrissy, I think. I can feel them on my side, too. "Thanks, Vicki," I say and really mean it. This is no time to hold a grudge.

Vicki smiles and puts her hand on my shoulder. I stand up a little straighter, take a deep breath, and walk around the corner into Grandpa's room.

His face lights up when he sees me. "Hey, it's my favorite granddaughter!"

I try to act relaxed and force a laugh. "You mean your *only* granddaughter."

Grandpa nods. "True. Aren't I a lucky guy? To what do I owe the honor of this visit from my favorite *and* only granddaughter?"

I don't have time to answer. Behind me there is a shuffle of feet, and I turn to see Vicki and TJ parting as Dad and Quinton come rushing into the room. Worry creases Dad's forehead.

"What is it?" he asks, looking from Grandpa to me and back again. "What happened?"

Grandpa shrugs. "Nothing. I'm doing great; walked clear to the end of the hall and back not more than an hour ago."

"Huh?" Dad says, clearly confused. He turns to me. "But on the phone you said there was an emergency."

I take an involuntary step toward the door, then catch myself and stop. "Oh, yeah, that," I say, wincing. "Maybe my . . . um . . . choice of words wasn't the best. I guess you thought I meant a medical emergency, huh?"

From the look on Dad's face, I figure I've got about four heartbeats before the fireworks start. At the same instant it occurs to me that I haven't really thought beyond this moment. How to begin the most important conversation of my life? I have no clue what the right thing to say might be, so I just blurt out the whole truth and nothing but the truth.

"I know why you two don't get along," I say. "And I have to tell you that I think it's silly to still be angry about something that happened *years* ago. It's time you both got over the war."

Dad and Grandpa gape at me, then at each other, then back at me. "The war?" Grandpa Ruben finally says. "What are you talking about, Cassie?"

I amp up the speed, talking fast. Get it all out on the table, *now*. "I read all about you being a hero in the Korean War, Grandpa," I say. "And how you saved people and got shot and earned medals, and all that. Then here comes Dad, and he is really, really against violence. I can see how you wouldn't understand, and be angry and all."

I gulp a big breath and turn to Dad. "I can see how Grandpa not understanding and getting mad would make you mad, too. So mad that you wouldn't even want to talk to him, or have us meet him, or be a fam—"

The word *family* catches in my throat, and for a second I think I'm going to cry. But I swallow hard and keep rolling, like Mom and Grandma Chrissy would want me to.

"We *are* a family, though," I say. "And we should act like one and let bygones be bygones. You know, forgive and forget, and all that stuff. So could you please—*please!*—shake hands and say I'm sorry?"

Grandpa Ruben's eyebrows are going up and down as fast as he keeps blinking. "Cassie, honey," he finally says, "your dad and I never had a problem over my military service in Korea. As far as I can remember, we never even discussed it. Besides, fact is I experienced war firsthand, and I hate it. It's mankind's worst invention. I'm glad to hear your dad's against it, too."

If words can be a wall, then I just ran headfirst into one. I'm stopped dead in my tracks. No war over the war? Really? I was so sure I had this figured out. . . .

Wait a minute now, maybe I do have this figured out, just minus the war part. "Okay," I say, "forget Korea. Would you please make up about Dad not becoming a farmer and not being here to harvest Grandma Chrissy's wheat?"

Now it's Dad's turn. "I always felt free to choose my own career path, Cassie. There was never an argument over my being an English teacher."

"That's right," Grandpa chimes in. "I'm the one who introduced him to Shakespeare. I've read all of the old bard's plays. Want to hear a few lines? I do a great Falstaff."

I'm beginning to feel a bit dizzy but shake it off and press on. "What about Dad moving to Oregon? Was that it? Did you want him to stay in Kentucky, Grandpa, and you two got into a fight over that?"

"I moved here to Kentucky from Tennessee when I was eighteen," Grandpa says. "Who am I to tell a man where he should live?"

"Did you two get into it over money, then?" I want to know. "Lots of families fall apart over money."

Dad shrugs. "We neither one of us have much of that. Nothing to argue about."

"Um . . ." I'm really grasping now. My theories are falling right and left. "Religion?"

"No."

"Politics?"

"No."

"Teenage rebellion?"

"No."

"Baseball? Are you a Yankees fan, Grandpa? Dad can't stand the Yankees."

"No. No. No."

"Well, *what* then?" I plead, out of ideas and desperate.

Dad focuses on the floor for a minute, then looks up at me, and his eyes have gone hard. In a cold whisper he says, "Your grandfather cheated me."

# 14. Do Not Pass Go

Grandpa's mouth falls open, and for a moment all he can do is sputter. Finally he finds his voice, and it comes out in a roar. "I didn't cheat you! You just couldn't stand getting beat, that's all!"

Dad goes crimson. If he were in a cartoon, there would be steam coming out of his ears. "Get beat? I didn't get beat. I got cheated! You rolled a four. You should have landed on Boardwalk. I had six hotels lined up there. The rent would have emptied your bank."

"Yes, *if* I had actually rolled a four," Grandpa shoots back. "But the dice hit your glass of iced tea and fell off the table. Everybody knows if that happens you get to roll again."

"Do not," Dad says. "You play the dice where they lie."

"Do too!" Grandpa insists. "You roll again."

"Do not!"

"Do too!"

"Do not!"

"Do too!"

"Do—"

"*Stop!*" The word explodes from my mouth so suddenly it catches even me by surprise. All heads snap in my direction.

"Do you mean to tell me," I say, unbelieving, "that you two haven't spoken to each other for all these years because of a game of . . . *Monopoly?*"

"No, Cassie," Vicki Higgins says, stepping between Dad and Grandpa. "It's not just because of Monopoly. Remember what I said at breakfast? As intelligent and loving as your father and grandfather may be, you're looking at what could be a pair of the stubbornest men on planet Earth."

"Hey, watch it now," Grandpa cautions, wagging a finger at her.

"Yeah," Dad says. "No need for personal insults."

Vicki Higgins looks Dad right in the eye. "If the truth is insulting, then so be it," she says. "I'm stubborn, too, but at least I admit it."

Now she's glaring at them both. "I reserve my

stubbornness, however, for things that actually matter, and Monopoly is *not* one of them."

Grandpa starts to protest, but Vicki raises her hand like a traffic cop and stops him cold. To me she says, "They're two peas in a pod, Cassie, no doubt butting heads over the silly things in life since the day your dad was born. An argument over a game of Monopoly was just one more in a long line, the straw that broke the camel's back, as the saying goes. They are both too *mule-headed* and *proud* to admit how *stupid* this all is and that they might actually be *wrong*."

"But I'm right," Grandpa says.

"No, *I'm* right," Dad quips back at him.

"I am!"

"No, I am!"

And they're off again, red-faced and arguing.

Vicki rolls her eyes so far back I think they might disappear. She throws up her hands. "See, Cassie? What did I tell you? Some things are better left alone!"

That's when it hits me, and despite all the strong feelings, my body goes weak. Because the truth is this: It doesn't matter what I do, or how hard I try to do it. Dad and Grandpa aren't going to make up.

There will be no perfect moment with us all sitting around a table, holding hands, laughing together, loving one another. That's the stuff of magazine covers and TV shows, and Hollywood movies, not real life. I was a naive little fool to think I could waltz in here and fix everything. Mom couldn't fix it. Grandma Chrissy couldn't fix it. Vicki Higgins can't fix it. And neither can I. My dream of a real family is completely and totally hopeless.

The end.

# 15. The Eye
## of the Storm

Tears well up in my eyes. Wiping furiously at them with the back of my hand, I turn away from the battling voices and stumble to the window.

I press my nose against the glass and look out over the hospital parking lot, across the highway, past Grandpa's farm, beyond the rolling landscape into the far distance. What I want more than anything right now is to be as far from all of this Kentucky craziness as I can get.

Home, that's where I belong. Oregon, way out west, two thousand miles and counting past the horizon and that line of dark clouds—

Whoa! Hold the phone! That's a major-looking storm. Even from this far away, I can see the gray smear of heavy rain.

I shudder, imagining how hard that downpour must be pounding everything in its path just like the day Mom died. Give it enough time, and it will be right on top of the farm and—

"Oh, no!" I shout. "Grandma's wheat!"

I whirl and sprint from the hospital room and around the corner to the elevator. I punch the DOWN button, then punch it again and again. C'mon! Grandpa said a big storm like that could knock wheat flat, soak it moldy, leave it in ruins. I've got to do . . . something. Now!

The elevator dings, and the door opens. I rush in and reach for the first-floor button. A hand beats me to it.

An old man's weathered, wrinkled hand.

I look up to see it belongs to Grandpa Ruben.

"You're going to need some help bringing that wheat in," he says as he hobbles in beside me.

Vicki Higgins is at one of Grandpa's elbows, lending support. TJ is at the other. The elevator starts to close.

"Hold!"

Another hand pops in and stops the door. It parts, and Dad hustles in with Quinton in tow.

Grandpa nods at Dad, pats Quinton on the head. "You ready to do some farming, kiddo?"

Quinton grins. "Yeah!"

"But Grandpa," I say, "what about your hip? Can you leave the hospital, just like that?"

He waves me off. "Don't worry, honey. The doctor said I need to work it a bit to promote the healing. I'm just following her orders."

Dad is shaking his head. "That's not what she meant, and you know it. If you're going to sneak out like this, you have to agree to just supervise the harvest, not actually work. And then you come straight back to the hospital as soon as we're done."

"Not straight back," Grandpa says. "You know we've got to—"

"Straight back," Dad insists.

"No."

"Yes."

"No."

"Yes."

"No."

Vicki Higgins does another eye roll. "Oh, Lordy," she says, "here we go again." To drown out the arguing she starts singing a Beach Boys tune, "Surf City."

"Mo-om!" TJ says, "does it *always* have to be classic rock?"

"Yes."

"No."

"Yes."

"No."

Quinton grins up at me. "Did you know that a pound of feathers is heavier than a pound of lead?"

For one clutch moment I consider jumping back out into the hall and running for it. I'm surrounded by loonies!

But the elevator door has already closed and—ready or not—we're all in this together, out of the gate, racing the coming storm.

# 16. A River of Mud

Dad drives the John Deere tractor like he was born on it, pulling Grandpa's old 12A combine smoothly around the first pass at the little wheat field.

TJ and I sit on a narrow metal bench on the combine, watching as a six-foot-wide swath of wheat stalks falls into the combine's mouth. Jiggle and thump, clamor and clang, what a noise! The 12A cuts and threshes, sends dust flying, and spits straw out the back.

But also there is grain, a golden shower of it, pouring into the hopper.

Grandma Chrissy's wheat.

"When I say go, you pull that lever," TJ yells over the bedlam.

"I know, you told me already!" I yell back. Three times he's told me. Heard the whole process; got it down pat.

First we have to transfer the wheat from the hopper into burlap sacks.

Then we close the sacks off with pieces of twine tied into a miller's knot. Which I also happen to have down pat, thank you very much.

Then we stop for just long enough to load the sacks into the back of Esmerelda, which Vicki Higgins is driving alongside us, still in her high heels. Grandpa is riding shotgun, leaning out the window, giving me the thumbs-up. Quinton is in the middle, talking a mile a minute, no doubt holding forth on the speed of light or some other immensely important Mr. Know-It-All made-up fact.

After Esmerelda is loaded, those three will take the sacks to the barn. Where Grandpa has sworn cross-his-heart that he will only supervise as Vicki and Quinton dump the wheat into the seed cleaner. A rattling, twitchy, gyrating thing—not unlike Quinton when he lip-synchs along with a CD—the cleaner will shake everything out the side except for those perfect little kernels of grain.

Everywhere there is noise by the ton and billowing clouds of khaki-colored dust that's so thick we all wear handkerchiefs over our noses and mouths. I'm dirty and getting dirtier by the minute. Streaked with sweat, too.

I feel like a farmer.

I love it.

Look at me, Mom! Look at us, Grandma Chrissy! We're doing it. We're working together. We're going to make it! We won't let you down! We're going to get this wheat in!

If we can just beat the storm, that is. I glance up to see how close the clouds are getting. Uh-oh. They're marching over the nearest hill like a giant wall of bad, bad news. I take a deep breath, push back my fear as best I can, and yell to everyone, "Hurry!"

No need. They've all seen it. Dad gives the old John Deere more gas. It roars and surges forward. The combine chews at the wheat and hurls grain into the hopper. We swing and turn back for another pass at the field. Then another. And another. Two, maybe three more to go.

The wind picks up, swirling dust into tiny tornadoes. I can smell rain just like the day Mom died. I would jump off this combine and run if it weren't for the voices of Mom and Grandma Chrissy in my ear.

"It's okay, Cassie. You can do it, girl."

Back and forth the combine cuts. Into the hopper the wheat pours. TJ and I keep pace, filling burlap sacks, then tying them off and loading them into the truck.

Now the wind whips in a frenzy, twisting the leaves on the trees, ripping some off, sending them spiraling. I cringe. The storm is almost on us, towering over the farm like a huge charcoal fist, rolling over itself to get at the wheat.

"Be brave," Mom and Grandma Chrissy say. "Keep going."

I swallow the panic rising in my throat, and bow my head to the work, trying with all of my might to block out the storm just as surely as it's blocking out the sun. It's a sprint to the finish. Harvest, Cassie! Harvest now!

One drop of rain puffs the farm lane dust.

Then five.

Then ten.

Then, as if someone ripped open the clouds, down come sheets of it, slashing on the crest of a roaring wind. In seconds the world turns to nothing but wet, the ground covered with rivers of mud.

In the safety of the barn, we all catch our breath and look at one another.

With smiles on our faces.

Which grow into grins.

Which burst into laughter.

And we slap one another on the back and share hugs and high fives, even Dad and Grandpa.

Because we made it. "By the skin of our teeth," Grandpa says.

Grandma Chrissy's wheat is in.

# 17. First Bread

Later, after the storm has passed and my heart has calmed back down, we all parade into the kitchen, following Grandpa. He's moving slowly and needs someone at each elbow to steady him, but he's smiling. In his arms he cradles a plastic bucket full of the new grain.

He puts it on the kitchen table, then says to all of us, "Gather round."

We do, Quinton, TJ, Vicki, and me.

Dad, too. He's still grumbling about getting Grandpa back to the hospital, but I can tell from his tone of voice that his protests are more for show than real.

This is just a theory, but I'm thinking that something about driving that tractor and bringing in the wheat under the storm's gun have taken the edge off him and Grandpa. They're both, after all, Kentucky farm boys at heart. Getting a crop in is what it's all about, at least for now.

Dad notices me eyeing him and stops the grumbling, then joins all of us in admiring the wheat.

Grandpa scoops a double handful from the bucket. "This is how we'll divide the entire crop," he says and makes a pile on the table. "The biggest part will be given, as Grandma Chrissy always insisted, to Food Share for those who are in need."

A second pile goes beside the first. "This goodly-sized portion I'll save for planting the next crop," Grandpa says. "And the rest . . ."

He lets the wheat flow through his fingers like some people would gold, making pile number three. "And the rest is for the old wheat grinder. Grandma Chrissy always said it made the best flour. Which, as you may have heard, makes the best bread."

Turns out Grandpa wasn't kidding when he called the grinder old. No electric motor to power the wheels, it's hand cranked.

We all take turns at it—Quinton first, since he's the youngest.

"Did you know," Quinton says as he works, "that Genghis Khan invented the hot dog?"

I ignore this silliness. I'm too busy watching the kernels of wheat go into the funnel at the top of the grinder hard and brown, and come out the bottom soft and tan.

Flour.

Finally it's my turn. I crank and crank and crank, loving the gritty sound of the wheels turning, the soothing feel, the earthy smell. Before I know it we've got a nice little mountain of powdered grain.

Dad pulls Grandma Chrissy's cookbook from the cupboard and lays it on the table. It's blue and frayed at the corners. Grandpa opens it to a marked page and turns it so I can see.

The paper is worn. Running my fingers over it, I can easily imagine Grandma Chrissy doing the same. At the top of the page I read, "First Bread." There you have it, the most important recipe in the whole wide world.

We set to work right away, gathering the tools Grandpa says we'll need and laying them out on the kitchen table: a big bowl front and center, a sifter, wooden spoons for mixing, a kneading board, a bread-loaf pan.

The ingredients come out next: milk, shortening, yeast, salt, baking soda, lukewarm water. And of course Grandma Chrissy's flour.

"Now we just follow the directions," Grandpa says. "It takes a while, what with waiting for the dough to rise then punching it down to rise again. And of course there is the baking." He smiles. "But it's worth it. Patience pays off. Just you wait. You've never had bread until you've had First Bread."

He eases himself into a chair and begins reading the recipe aloud. "Number one: Scald the milk and pour into a deep bowl. Number two: Meanwhile soften the yeast. . . ."

Next thing you know the pace has picked up. Everybody is reading the recipe. "Sift the flour. . . ." "Add to yeast. . . ." "Stir!" We're all hustling around the kitchen, elbowing in, laughing, getting the job done. In a blink we've got dough!

We slow down now, taking turns kneading the soft mix the way Grandpa showed us, folding it in, then pushing away with the heels of our hands in a sort of rocking motion. When it's just right, we place the dough gently into the loaf pan and cover it with a soft, clean dish towel so the yeast can do its magic in private and make it rise.

Then we wait.

And wait.

And wait.

"Let's play a game!" Quinton suggests.

Vicki nods. "Monopoly would be fun."

It's only after a very long moment of uncomfortable silence that she rolls her eyes and says, "Just kidding, y'all. C'mon! Can't you take a joke? We might as well play hot potato with a stick of lit dynamite."

Instead we play Name That Tune. And Twenty Questions. And Charades. Quinton keeps peeking under the dish towel to check on the dough. Finally he says, "It's rising!"

Grandpa shows Quinton how to punch the dough down, which he loves, acting like he's in a kung-fu movie. Grandpa whistles the "1812 Overture," then demonstrates how to rub his head and pat his belly at the same time, then switch. Dad shakes his head, but I can see a smile playing around the corners of his mouth.

After what seems like forever, the dough is ready for the oven. I put it in, while Vicki Higgins tells us about the time her casserole exploded in the microwave. "Blew the door open and flung cheese all over the kitchen! Lucky for me I was taking a bubble bath."

Dad and Grandpa and Quinton and I think it's a funny story, but TJ says, "See what I have to live with?"

Grandpa tells us about the very first time he and Grandma Chrissy planted the very first crop of wheat. "She toiled right alongside me in the field. Boy, you talk about work! She was a strong, good woman." And how much he and Grandma Chrissy loved being farmers. "We were proud of being able to feed people. We knew we were contributing."

As he talks, the kitchen fills with the smell of baking bread, and my mouth starts to water.

Finally the timer bell rings. Dad opens the oven door and pulls out the most beautiful loaf of bread ever.

"Here, Cassie," Grandpa says, handing me Grandma Chrissy's old wood-handled bread knife. "You do the honors."

I cut a slice for everyone and quickly nab some butter from the refrigerator, plus grape jelly for Quinton.

Grandpa says, "Before we eat we must give thanks. Let's join hands." He reaches out to take mine. On a sudden impulse I hop a quick step back, and instead Grandpa is reaching for Dad.

Both men stop short.

"I'll stand . . . uh, over there," I say and dart around the table and slip in beside Vicki. She gives me a quick wink, like Mom used to do, and I wink back, feeling pretty clever. It's not until Quinton starts giggling that I realize I'm now going to have to hold hands with TJ.

But when Dad reaches out and takes Grandpa's hand, I don't care. The sacrifice is worth it. It's all I can do to keep myself from shouting *woo-hoo!* Look at us, Mom, holding hands in a circle! Look at us, Grandma Chrissy, just like you would want us to be!

After Grandpa says a prayer, he smiles and holds his piece of bread up. "To Grandma Chrissy," he says.

We raise our slices of bread and repeat, "To Grandma Chrissy!" Together we all take a big, wonderful, perfect bite. . . .

"Uh-oh," Vicki mumbles through her mouthful. "Too much salt."

"*Way* too much," Grandpa agrees, a pained expression on his face. "We goofed."

Quinton is the first one to spit his bread out. "*Ack!*" he says. "That's terrible!"

"Quinton!" I scold, ready to lay into him for saying such a rude thing about Grandma Chrissy's bread.

But taste buds don't lie. For once in Mr. Know-It-All's harebrained little life, he's completely, totally right.

# 18. The Question of Perfection

I, of course, want to jump right in and start over. "It'll still be First Bread," I insist, "just a second try."

But Quinton says he's hungry *now* and has to eat, "or I'll die!"

Grandpa lays a hand on Quinton's shoulder. "I'm hungry, too," he says. "Grandma Chrissy wouldn't mind if we work on the bread later. How does pizza sound in the meantime?"

"Good idea," Dad says, and before I can get over the shock of them actually agreeing on something, Vicki hooks my elbow and ushers us all out the door, into cars, and down the farm lane toward town.

Gathered around Grandpa's hospital bed, we hold hands again, then toast Grandma Chrissy with slices of pepperoni and cheese pizza, and wash it down with Coke.

Which, I have to say, isn't exactly the perfection I have been imagining all this time.

Especially when Dad and Grandpa start arguing again, this time over who will win the World Series.

Vicki rolls her eyes and starts making wisecracks about men.

This, of course, sets TJ off. "Mo-om!"

Quinton, not to be outdone, says to me, "Did you know that in caveman days they used straws as vacuum cleaners?" He demonstrates by sucking pizza crumbs up off the bedspread, then blowing them in my face.

Back home in Oregon it's no better. True, Grandpa calls almost every day. Or we call him.

Which is nice.

Out of the hospital, he's staying with Vicki and TJ. Where, according to Vicki, he's been trying to get Tom Turkey to eat the salty bread—no luck—and supervising the restoration of her breakfast nook, which is driving the workers crazy.

That's nice, too, if you're not one of the workers.

But he and Dad disagree on any- and everything, and sometimes Dad hangs up and says he doesn't know why he even bothers.

Which isn't exactly the perfection I have been imagining, either.

Still, we *are* going back to Kentucky for Thanksgiving. And Grandpa is considering coming out to Oregon for Christmas. Plans are in the works for harvesting Grandma Chrissy's wheat crop next summer, too. And Dad has promised to teach me how to drive the old John Deere.

Best of all, there are three loaves of First Bread in the freezer, and one on the kitchen counter. We finally got the recipe right. (One quarter the salt makes all the difference.)

Holding the old wood-handled bread knife Grandpa gave me, I can feel Grandma Chrissy and Mom beside me, their warm hearts filling the room. I carefully cut slices for Dad, Quinton, and me. Into the toaster they go, and quickly the kitchen and then the whole house fills with that wonderful smell. When the toast pops up, I put it on a plate and serve us all around. A bit of butter spread smooth. We all take deep breaths, then dig in.

"Mmm," Dad murmurs. "Good bread!"

"Woo-hoo!" says Quinton and whirls out of control, crash-landing in the trash can *again*.

I smile and take another bite. Perfection? No, but close enough.

Tom Birdseye is the author of such popular books for young readers as *Attack of the Mutant Underwear*, a Georgia Children's Book Award finalist, a Louisiana Young Readers' Choice Award nominee, and a Sunshine State Young Reader's Award Master List title; *Tarantula Shoes*; and *Just Call Me Stupid*. *Booklist* has observed, "Birdseye hits young adolescent concerns right on the mark." He lived in Kentucky for many years, working on farms after school and in the summers, but now he resides with his family in Oregon. You can find out more about him on his website at www.tombirdseye.com.